ZANIB MIAN
ILLUSTRATED BY KYAN CHENG

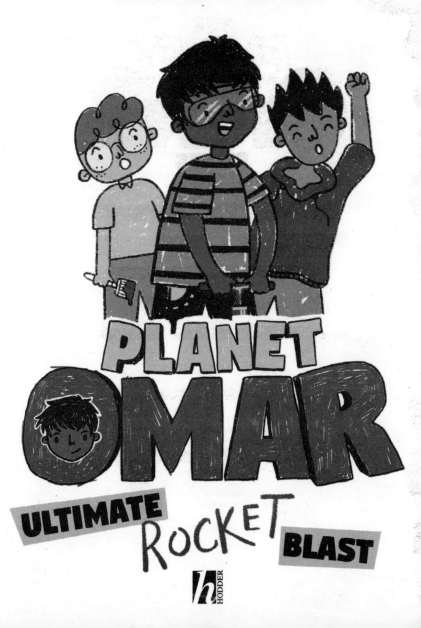

PLANET OMAR

ULTIMATE ROCKET BLAST

HODDER

HODDER CHILDREN'S BOOKS

First published in Great Britain in 2022 by Hodder & Stoughton

1 3 5 7 9 10 8 6 4 2

A CIP catalogue record for this book
is available from the British Library.

ISBN 978 1 444 96100 3

Printed and bound in Great Britain by
Clays Ltd, Elcograf S.p.A

The paper and board used in this book
are made from wood from responsible sources.

MIX
Paper from
responsible sources
FSC
www.fsc.org
FSC® C104740

Hodder Children's Books
An imprint of
Hachette Children's Group
Part of Hodder & Stoughton Limited
Carmelite House
50 Victoria Embankment
London, EC4Y 0DZ

An Hachette UK Company
www.hachette.co.uk

www.hachettechildrens.co.uk

For my brother, Hamza, the rocket scientist.

OMAR

I love science, just like my parents

I will do (almost) anything for my best friends

I've always dreamed of taking a rocket ride

I have a love/hate relationship with my big sister, Maryam

Mr PHILPOT

MUM

Quite a fun mum, but never let her know
An AMAZING scientist
Loves crime novels
Pushes me to see the best in others

BURRRRR

CHAPTER 1

RRRRP!

That wasn't me. It was my best friend, Charlie.

We were sitting around his grandma's table for tea. It was a special invite and she had baked fresh scones, without actually realising that Charlie, Daniel and I had made a pact to hate scones for ever after Daniel nearly choked on a particularly dry one last month.

But she had LOTS of fizzy drinks, which Charlie was filling up on, hence the super-loud burp.

'Honey blossom!' said his grandma crossly. 'You should never burp at the table. In fact, you should never, ever burp!'

Charlie blushed, but I don't think it was because of the burp. He hated it when his grandma called him cute names in front of us.

'That's impossible,' our other best friend, Daniel, declared, spraying Jammie Dodger crumbs all over his white top.

'No, it's not. Back in the day, a gentleman never used to burp. Not once. I don't know what's happened to the humans of today,' she said.

'Sorry, Granny,' said Charlie.

'It's OK, Buttercup. Just never, ever do it again,' replied Granny. She was the only person I knew who carried on using loving terms for people she was mad at.

I wanted to say that Daniel was right. Burps were necessary. You couldn't not ever burp again. I read somewhere that if you weren't able to burp, they came out as **bottom burps** and if you somehow held everything in, your stomach would literally burst. But I had to be polite, so I kept quiet, unlike my brain, which was imagining Charlie's granny swelling up into a balloon-bellied old lady from keeping all her burps in.

Daniel wasn't remembering his manners. He
chucked down a whole glass of fizzy and let
out the **most GINORMOUS
whopper of a COLOSSAL BURP**
I had ever heard.

He clapped both hands over his mouth right
away and looked at Granny with sorry eyes, but

also said, 'Did you hear that? **IT WAS O... !**
I almost flew into the wall with the power of
that burp!'

Charlie and I exploded into giggles as
Granny shook her head in disbelief.

After we helped clear up, Daniel asked, 'Hey,
Buttercup, if your granny calls you names like
that when she's cross, what does she call you
when she's happy with you?'

'Argh, you don't want to know,' said Charlie,
in a whisper.

'I'll have to ask your granny where she got that fizzy stuff from. I want to burp like that for the rest of my life!'

'Did it hurt?' Charlie asked.

'It did a bit. But it was worth it,' Daniel said with the kind of twinkle in his eyes that mums and dads have when they talk about how proud they are of their kid.

'She only has it on special occasions,' said Charlie, 'and she'll probably never let me have it again after that!'

'Sorry!' Daniel grinned.

I looked at my watch. It was only 4 p.m. The whole weekend was passing slower than normal, even though time usually raced

by when I was with my best friends. But it was super slow because I was waiting for something to happen. Our teacher, Mrs Hutchinson, had left us with a massive cliffhanger on Friday.

'Next week, I have some **EXCITING NEWS TO DO WITH ROCKETS!'**

Mrs H had said. And she wouldn't say a word more, which obviously had my imagination spinning into overdrive with all the possible things that could be. I was sure she and her very rich uncle and friend of the school, Lancelot Macintosh, must have organised a rocket ride for us! And I was bursting to find out if I was right.

CHAPTER 2

I was wrong. You knew I was going to be wrong, didn't you?

It was too crazy, even with my imagination, to think that we'd be having a rocket ride. Most kids haven't had a ride in a supercar, let alone a rocket.

'Only astronauts get to go in rockets,' my big sister, Maryam, had teased me.

But sometimes unexpected things do happen, don't they?

'Hey, if Omar wants to be an astronaut when he grows up, I'm cool with that.' Dad had winked.

And Mum had said that even if it wasn't a rocket ride, anything to do with rockets would be amazing anyway.

And she was right!

On Monday morning, Mrs Hutchinson whizzed through the register like she was bursting to get to the news. Then, with clumps of her wavy hair flying like rockets in different directions, she told us we were going to be taking

part in a **NATIONAL ROCKET-BUILDING COMPETITION**

'Cool. Super cool. Cool, cool, way cool!' I said.

'That sounds totally awesome,' added Charlie, his eyebrows jumping up and down like they were on a trampoline.

'Well, I'm no rocket scientist,' said Daniel, 'but if you want it made out of paper,

I CAN ORIGAMI THE CAULIFLOWER OUT OF IT.

And he was right, of course, because one of the many surprising things about Daniel is that he can make almost anything with origami.

We listened carefully to the rest of the information Mrs H gave us:

- The national rocket-building competition was organised by MXF Labs, an independent space agency who are going to land a human-less rocket on Mars.

- We didn't have to take part, but if we did, the school would support us fully.

- Only one group from the school would eventually take part in the national competition. We would have a mini school competition to see who got through. Yikes!

- We had two weeks to research and prepare our rockets (basically figure out how to build one).

• Then we had to go to MXF Labs' private grounds in Surrey for a night and day, where all the participants would build their rockets and compete to see which rocket won!

'You can make teams of three or four to work on this,' announced Mrs H.

'YESSSSSSS!' I screamed.

Three is the magic number. It means Charlie, Daniel and I can be on one team. It's horrible every time we get asked to pair up to work on something.

The three of us look at each other silently,

wondering who is going to make a sacrifice and work with someone else. Then we watch the hero walk off, as if he's going into an exploding building.

When this happens, Daniel always tries to be the hero.

'I'll go,' he says, as if he's about to donate an organ. And like he feels that he simply can't put either me or Charlie through it.

But we always make sure we sort of take it in turns to work together.

We had loads of questions, so we completely hijacked Mrs H's lunchtime. But she had been expecting it and welcomed it with a

chatting to us while she rubbed her tummy. She was going to be having a baby soon.

'This will be great for you friends.' **She** winked. 'And Omar, I am sure your parents will be a huge help with the planning!'

'Is that cheating, though? If both of your parents are scientists and they help you?' I asked.

'No. The rules say you can have some guidance from adults at the planning stage, but then you have to put it together yourself on the day with supervision.'

'Cool!' Daniel grinned. 'Let's hope every other kid has parents who are bad at science.'

'Oh, Mrs H. You forgot to tell us what the prize is!' said Charlie.

'Ah yes. I have a feeling you'll love this – the winning group get to have a tour of MXF Labs' rocket, H8!'

'WOOOAAAAH!'
I screamed.

It wasn't a rocket ride. But it was still pretty much a dream come true.

I was dying to get home and tell Mum and Dad.

CHAPTER 3

Mum and Dad were really **GETTING THEIR GEEK ON** once I filled them in on the competition.

'Right, so you have two weeks to come up with the **BEST HOMEMADE ROCKET CONCEPT** the world has ever seen!' said Dad.

'Better brush up on Newton's laws of motion.' Mum winked back at him and they had a **super cheesy chuckle,** while

Maryam and I wondered what they were going

on about.

My little brother, Esa, announced that he

was a rocket and flew off the table, landing

straight in Dad's arms. Dad sure can predict an

Esa move when it's coming!

Maryam doesn't like science as much

as I do. She likes poems and arty

stuff, but for some crazy reason – probably to completely destroy the excitement everyone was feeling – she said, '*I WANT TO BE ON YOUR TEAM, OMAr.*'

The reason I KNOW she didn't actually want to and was only asking to get me in trouble with Mum and Dad if I said no was because she said it with one hand on her hip and one eyebrow raised up high.

She had forgotten that I am the **king of reading eyebrows.** I practically wrote a book about it with Charlie and his eyebrows as my inspiration, because Charlie's eyebrows do a lot of speaking for him.

I glared back at her, imagining the high eyebrow as a very hairy, squiggly worm, when Mum shouted, '**N°O°O°O°O°O!**'

Huh? Is Mum answering for me and not letting annoying Maryam help? How did that happen? I thought.

We all spun round to look at her. She was on her phone.

'NO. NO. Noooo. Silly autocorrect or whatever does that!' she was saying.

'What happened, darling?' her hero (my dad) (yuck) asked.

'I was asking my new lab assistant how her son Sayan is, but his name got **autocorrected** to **SĀTĀN** . So, I typed it again and it corrected to **SĀTĀN** without asking me! And I did it again and now it just says: HOW'S SATAN? SATAN. SATAN. Oh my Lord, she's going to think I'm a weirdo or that I'm being mean to her because she's new!'

Obviously, we all found this autocorrect disaster hilarious and rolled around on the floor laughing our brains out while Mum got cross and said it wasn't funny.

HA

HA

'Right ...' Dad breathed through giggles. 'Let's chat to the other parents and get this rocket rolling. But let's not text them. That's clearly a dangerous game.'

HA

HA!

I guess I had expected that my parents would want us to win so they would just go ahead and create the rocket with their super-fantastic science brains. But they decided to use some sort of crafty parenting technique where we had to do our best to come up with a plan for a rocket all by ourselves.

'This is what we've been preparing you for all your life, with SCIENCE SUNDAYS they said.

But we really had no clue where to start, let alone how to win this thing.

CHAPTER 4

Obviously, the three of us couldn't wait until the evening to get started. The rocket – our rocket – was all we could talk about at school the next day.

'It's going to be EPIC!' said Daniel, rubbing out his drawing of a motorbike and starting again, for the eleventh time. We were having an art lesson, and Mrs

Hutchinson had asked us to draw what we last dreamt of.

'I can't wait to get started on reading up on how to make one ...' I said, drifting into daydreams of how rockets would work in a fantasy world.

Maybe a **thousand baby dragons** would sit inside and blow magical fire out the bottom to send it flying up. Or just one big one, like my imaginary dragon, H_2O.

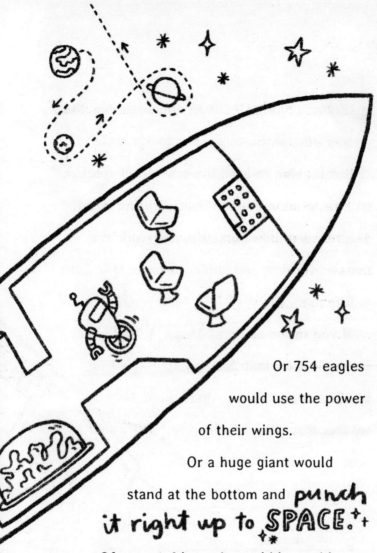

Or 754 eagles

would use the power

of their wings.

Or a huge giant would

stand at the bottom and *punch*

it right up to SPACE.

Of course, I knew it would be nothing

like that in real life.

'We have to name it.' Charlie beamed.

'Super definitely!' Daniel and I said together.

Mrs Hutchinson came over to our table to tell us that Mr Philpot, the school's IT teacher, had a special interest in physics, so he was the one who would be supporting any kids that decided to enter and joining them at MXF Labs on the day.

If you remember how **SCARY** Mr Philpot is, you'll know that this was definitely the LEAST fun part of the whole thing. He's the teacher who shouts so loud that the whole school building shakes.

Today, he was going to be meeting all the rocket makers to get them started. There were only four groups of kids from our school entering, mostly because:

1. I think many kids are secretly scared of science. Especially rocket science.

2. Only Years 5 and 6 could enter (phew – that's what I can tell Maryam if she ever asks to be in our group again).

The other groups were from different classes. So when Mr Philpot and his giant sandals came, Charlie, Daniel and I

were the only kids on the table with him to talk about our first steps to making a rocket. He talked about rockets the same way he talked about everything else, as if making one would be as **boring** as trying to open a webpage on a slow Internet connection. I figured out this was just the way he talked and he couldn't help that all the words ejected out of his mouth were in the same tone and at the same pace, no matter what he was saying.

blah blah blah

Oh, except when he was shouting, of course. Then he was capable of lots of excitement.

Mr Philpot explained about the mini competition, which made me **scared and EXCITED** all at the same time. We might never even get to MXF Labs! But if we did, it meant we had already won a little bit!

While we were told we'd have to start with some research before we could try to make test rockets, Ellie and Sarah had been having their own whispery conversation, with regular looks towards us and rather **cruel-sounding GIGGLES.**

Eventually, when Mr Philpot left, they decided to spark up mischief.

'You guys do know that your rocket will **EPICALLY FLOP** if you have Daniel on your team?' Ellie asked.

'Yes. Super duh. You need brains for rocket

science,' Sarah pitched in.

They giggled.

'And in case you didn't notice ... erm ... Daniel doesn't really have any?' Ellie drove the point home while the three of us stared at them in horror.

I couldn't believe that words so mean could come out of a human's mouth. And right in front of poor Daniel.

I looked at Charlie, who was doing his fish impersonation again, opening and closing his mouth as if to say something, but being completely stuck for words.

Daniel was going red and definitely about to erupt. I knew I had to stop the eruption rather than think of something smart to say to Sarah and Ellie ... but it was too late. With a roaring

'ARGHHHHH'

Daniel launched the heavy, metal stapler

straight into the fish tank.

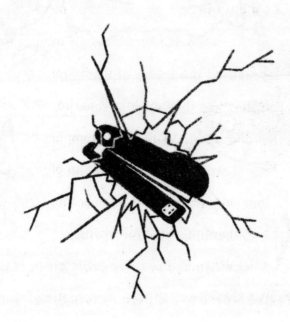

CHAPTER 5

Daniel realised the horror of what
he had done, as time went in slow
motion and we all watched the fish
tank shatter and eight little fish
land in puddles on the floor.

I couldn't believe the bad
luck fish had in our school! A fish tank
had broken in a different class before with
rumours that it was Mr Philpot's shouting that

had done it, not to mention

the **FiSH in THe jelly Pond disaster!**

Mrs Hutchinson's hair suddenly looked electrocuted in panic, but she tried to keep calm and get us all away from the broken bits of glass.

'I'll go and get the caretaker,' said Charlie, as he scooped up the poor fish and plonked them into his water bottle (which I hope he will never ever drink out of again!).

He was very good in emergencies.

Daniel was now shaking like a leaf.

'I'm so sorry, miss. I'm so sorry.'

He had snapped right out of the **GRiPS OF THE MONSTER**

that had made him do it. As if it wasn't really this Daniel standing in front of us that had thrown the stapler.

I went to put my arm around him and hoped he couldn't hear that my own heart was beating wildly in my chest – terrified of the punishment my best friend would get for this.

Would he still be allowed to enter the competition?

That evening, when we got together at Daniel's house for a research session, Daniel was a complete mess. He was going to have to wait till the next day to see Mr McLeary and find out what punishment had been decided for him. We spent most of the two hours we had calming Daniel down as he lay with his face in the carpet.

'You haven't been in trouble at school for ages. They won't be that hard on you,' said Charlie. 'And at least Sarah and Ellie didn't get away with it this time. Mrs Hutchinson said they aren't allowed to have their morning break and they have to sharpen all the pencils instead.'

'Yes, but they don't have to go see Mr McSCARY! And I do!' wailed Daniel. 'And they're probably right, I am stupid, aren't I?

'No!' Charlie and I said together.

'And Mr McLeary can be really kind ... er, sometimes ... erm.' I coughed.

'What if he's not? What if he doesn't let me make the rocket?'

'He will,' we said.

'What if he **BANISHES** me from school for ever?!' Daniel wasn't even listening to us any more.

'He can't!' we said.

'WHAT IF HE EATS ME ALIVE!?'

I'll never see my mum and dad and my little
sister again!'

'Come on, Daniel, none of that will happen,'
I said, trying to pull him up by the back of his
T-shirt, which made a little RIPPING sound.

'Arrghhh! I could have died, Omar!' said
Daniel.

And then he burst out into good old Daniel
giggles at his own ridiculousness.

'OK. I will get through this,' he breathed to
himself. 'I am GOOD, I am KIND,
I am ME.'

Charlie and I watched Daniel say this to
himself a few times, with his eyes closed. I
knew his parents were teaching him new things
to keep calm when things got rotten.
We only shared amused smiles twice, which I

feel bad for because even though it made me want to laugh a little bit, it worked. It helped my friend. Daniel was ready to talk **ROCKETS.**

First, we turned to our good old pal, Google.

We always refer to Google as if he were an old friend. We'd say things like,

'Remember that time Google told us

horror stories?'

'Remember when Google helped us with our homework?'

'Remember when we got lost and Google helped us find our way home?'

This time we asked our pal to show us how rockets work. We knew what to search for because Dad had said, 'Hey, kids. Remember, before you start trying to make a rocket, you need to know the science behind how they work. That's your first step.'

Mum had winked and Maryam had rolled her eyes and said, 'SUPER NERDY.'

Daniel's mum was bringing in some food for us to chomp on while we worked.

'Guys. I'm saying sorry already, because I KNOW my mum's cooking is awful. That's why Dad normally cooks. And Omar, that's why I try to

eat at your house as often as
possible.'

'I do too.' Charlie giggled.
'I like samosas the best.'

'Thanks, Charlie, but those are a treat. We
basically only get them in Ramadan
and on Eids.'

'That rice stuff with the meat in it is good
too. Like a million happy flavours in my mouth,'
said Daniel.

'That's biriyani and yup,
it's my favourite.' I
smiled.

Daniel's mum
came and put some
plates down in front
of us and smiled.

'Thanks, Mrs Green,' I said.

'You're welcome, boys. Enjoy my vegan stew.'

Vegan, I thought. Cool. I wouldn't have to ask if the meat was halal. I think Mrs Green knows **I only eat halal, vegetarian or vegan food,** but I still ask and I feel extra shy when I have to. But vegan was safe.

Daniel scooped a spoonful into his mouth. I was a bit worried about the dribble of gravy falling off the spoon, but it didn't matter because seconds later, the whole spoonful was sprayed everywhere.

'EWWWWWW. It tastes like **hippo breath!'** spat Daniel. 'Oh my gosh, no, it tastes like a Brussels sprout's B.O.'

'I'm not hungry!' Charlie said, quickly pushing his plate away.

'I ate before coming,' I fibbed.

'Don't worry, I won't make you eat it,' said Daniel.

But we couldn't hurt Mrs Green's feelings, so we either had to EAT it or ... flush it down the toilet to look as if we ate it!

We chose the second option. I felt so BAD about that. It was wasting food while others didn't have any. And even if no one ever found out, Allah knew. He knows everything. I regretted it as soon as we pressed the flush. But we couldn't bring it back, so I had to live with what we did.

We carried on with hungry bellies and found out a man called **Isaac Newton** from like a thousand years ago made up some 'laws' that are so important that they are still behind rocket science and other cool stuff today.

This is what he looked like:

'Is his hair a wig?' asked Charlie.

'Dunno,' I said.

'I need one,' said Charlie.

'Ohhhhh, that's why the name is so familiar. He's the guy who discovered gravity when an apple fell on his head!' I remembered.

'Super cool,' said Charlie. 'I wonder how he felt it through all that hair.'

Newton's third law (he has two others about moving objects) says that every ACTION has an EQUAL and OPPOSITE REACTION.

If you slam a book down on a table, it bounces back up a bit because the table pushes back. So, if a rocket can push against the ground with the force of hot gases made by burning rocket fuel, the ground will push back just as hard and the rocket will move upwards. It's just an EQUAL and OPPOSITE REACTION like Newton described.

'Oh WOW! Yes, he's right, that funny man with a wig,' said Daniel. 'Remember that uh-maze-ing burp I did at Charlie's gran's house? I felt the power of the gases push me backwards! If it wasn't for the wall, I would have ended up in her back garden!'

'But you didn't actually move backwards.' Charlie giggled.

'Yes, like I said, if it wasn't for the wall!' Daniel laughed. 'And don't even get me started on the **ROCKET-POWERED fart** I managed the other day after I was made to eat Brussels sprouts. We should just fill our rocket with fizzy drinks and the world's most fartiest foods.'

Charlie and Daniel laughed uncontrollably, enjoying this thought and listing foods in order of 'fart power':

Chickpeas

Cabbage

Baked Beans

Brussel Sprouts

Daal

I giggled too. But not as much as usual. My mind was on trying to make this rocket the best it could be. We needed to get serious and think. **I NEEDED that prize!** We had already wasted too much time.

I wondered if Ellie and Sarah were right.

Would Daniel hold us back? Then I immediately

felt GUiLTY for being mean to my friend in

my head.

CHAPTER 6

The next day at school, Daniel had to visit Mr McScary, our head teacher, in his office.

'It's time for you to go, Daniel,' announced Mrs Hutchinson across the room.

Daniel's eyes **popped out of his face**

as he stared at us. 'My legs won't move. They've forgotten how to work!'

'It's OK, Daniel. Remember the time I had to have my lunches in there with him. I made it through. You will too!' I said.

'You are good. You are kind. You are you!' encouraged Charlie.

Daniel used his hands, pushing them on to the table to launch himself off his chair. It reminded me of our neighbour, Mrs Rogers, who does that because her legs aren't so strong any more. And I figured out it was using **Newton's laws** too.

We watched him slowly walk towards the door and give us one last dramatic look before he left.

'Do you think we'll ever see him again?' I said to Charlie.

'Nope,' said Charlie. 'He went Hulk on a fish tank!'

We could only joke while we waited with big lumps in our throats for the verdict.

Daniel came back pretty quickly with a bounce in his step.

PHEW!

We knew from the way he opened the door that all was OK.

'He went SO easy on me!' said Daniel, slipping back into his seat. 'He said he was proud I was taking part in the rocket competition and he is confident I will grow.'

'What? Like grow upwards?' said Charlie.

'I guess,' said Daniel, shrugging his shoulders. 'But all kids do that, don't they? So it's a bit funny.'

'I think he means as a person. My mum talks about growing, like learning from your mistakes and becoming better,' I said.

'Aaaaaah,' said Daniel.

And then he went to give Mrs Hutchinson a

high-five. We all knew she had something to do with how easy McScary went on Daniel.

During our next rocket session, we actually got down to business. But the business was really hard. I mean – it's **ROCKET SCIENCE!**

We got that we needed to create a force that would **push down** on the ground to **push our rocket upWards,** but we had no idea what it could be.

We watched some videos about rocket science, but all the demonstrations used **DANGEROUS CHEMICALS.** This competition had lots of rules about safety and we were pretty sure that we couldn't get hold of some of this stuff even if we wanted. One guy used real jet-engine fuel!

'How do they expect us to make rockets when we

can't use or get any of the stuff?!' said Charlie.

We sat there, helpless, all three of us almost in tears. It was too hard. Think about the hardest thing you've ever had to figure out and then multiply it by a thousand. No, a million, or actually probably a gazillion!

'We have to present our ideas to Mr Philpot tomorrow!' I wailed.

'Ellie and Sarah will never let us hear the end of it!' said Charlie.

Daniel looked super stressed at the mention of our classmates.

'You have to beg your parents to do it for us!' pleaded Charlie.

'They won't ...' I said.

'That's why you have to BEG,' said Daniel.

'Yeah. Pester power.' Charlie grinned.

I imagined myself with a really big brain that could figure this out without my parents' help. It was too big to fit in the small skull I have, so I had to imagine myself with a much bigger

head. The much-
bigger-headed Omar
toppled over when he
tried to walk.

'OK ... I'll ask my
parents,' I decided.

I had really wanted them to be proud of
me. Proud that I managed to do rocket science
all by myself with my friends. I hoped they
wouldn't be disappointed that I couldn't figure
it out.

So as we all sat down for dinner, with Mrs
Rogers joining us as she often does, I pushed
my food (which happened to be quite highly
fart-powered) around my plate and braced
myself to sheepishly admit that my friends

and I were pretty stuck. That I, Omar, son of scientists, was an epic flop.

'What's wrong with your face?' Maryam asked. 'You look like you accidently swallowed a fly and then did something stupid like swallow a frog to go and get it.'

Everyone stopped eating and looked at me.

'Erm ... we still don't know how to make a rocket ...' I pushed the confession out of my mouth.

'Oh!' Mum laughed. 'Is that it, sweetie? Of course you don't! It's rocket science! It's not supposed to be easy, and we weren't expecting you'd have the whole thing figured out this soon.'

'Really?' I blurted. 'I thought you'd be really disappointed in me.'

'We are,' said Maryam.

'Ignore her!' said Mrs Rogers and put her broccoli on Maryam's plate while she wasn't looking.

'You're being too hard on yourself, kid,' said Dad, slapping my back. 'Do you know how long we take figuring stuff out at work? Sometimes years!'

'So tell us what you've done so far and where the trouble is,' said Mum.

Charlie, Daniel and I told them we used our pal Google to look stuff up. I explained all about Newton and his laws and that rockets have fuel called propellant. Daniel said how all the propellants are **SUPER DANGER⊗US** for kids, so we needed something that would create a big enough force to lift our rocket really high off the ground.

'Wow. Good stuff!' said Mum.

'Rocket scientists in the making!' Dad high-fived me. 'You've clearly understood how it works, boys.'

I blushed happily, and shyly looked down at my **Fart - POWERED FOOD.** The boost from my parents gave me some sort of brain energy because right then I realised something ...

Mum's voice was coming in through my brain wave. 'Yes, but

don't think too big, sweeties, think smaller ...'

'Think home ingredients!' I blurted. 'We need to ask Google in a different way!'

'Yes! Remember your pal Google will only answer what you ask it.' Dad winked.

But Charlie was still scrunching his eyebrows at me in worry and Daniel was kicking me under the table, so I added, 'If you guys ... erm ... just made it for us, we would win ... and nobody would know really that it was actually your rocket.' I showed them all my teeth, to somehow make what I said seem less bad.

'Omar, even if nobody knew, Allah would know. God knows everything we do. All our secrets.'

'I know ...' I said sheepishly. 'It's just I'm so desperate for that rocket tour. It's my dream!'

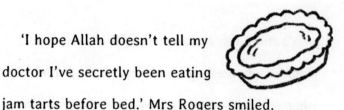

'I hope Allah doesn't tell my doctor I've secretly been eating jam tarts before bed.' Mrs Rogers smiled.

Mum and Dad chuckled at this and I quickly shovelled the rest of my dinner down my throat. 'Please can we go and google something now?'

'Sure,' said Dad.

We shot up the stairs.

'If there's one thing I know how to do, it's watching YouTube,' Charlie said and found some videos for us to watch. 'These water rockets look so easy and we don't need any chemicals!'

I high-fived him. '**YESSSSSS, Charlie!** And there's the vinegar and baking soda rockets too!'

'Sorry I didn't come up with something helpful,' Daniel said, holding up his fingers for us to see his nails chewed right down to the skin. 'I was only productive at chewing my nails away with worry.'

I knew he was nervous about the other kids in the class teasing him again, perhaps leading to another eruption that McScary might not forgive this time.

'It's OK, Daniel. I have a plan for you.' I winked at him.

CHAPTER 7

Mr Philpot came to our class and sat down
for the meeting to hear our ideas, which went
pretty well, much to the dismay of Sarah and
Ellie, whose eyebrows **furrowed
deeper and deeper** into their
foreheads as they listened.

My cheeky plan played out superbly and also
backfired in our faces at the same time. You
might be wondering how that is even possible ...

Last night, Charlie and I got Daniel
to rehearse a few lines to say to Mr
Philpot, so that the girls would overhear
and think he was really smart.

'Any time you want to say "water",
call it **"dihydrogen
monoxide"**,' I said, elbowing Charlie
with extreme pride.

'What-the-floxide?' said Daniel.

'Dihydrogen monoxide,' I repeated
encouragingly.

'Why ... hydrogen ... peroxide,'
tried Daniel.

'"Di", like if you were dead you would
die,' said Charlie. 'Then "hydrogen", then
"monoxide", as in "mon" from the beginning of
"Monday".'

'Oh, OK ... die ... hydrogen, die!' said Daniel through giggle fits.

Daniel was hilarious!

'It's OK, I'm kidding, I've got it – die ... hydrogen ... mon ... oxide. Dihydrogen monoxide!'

And so, we spent the meeting trying to sound like cool rocket scientists for the rest of the class.

Mr Philpot shook his head and said things like, 'Right. Aha. HMMM. OK, great!'

Sarah and Ellie tried their best to pretend they didn't even notice how smart we sounded, by looking busy with their reading books.

Then at the end, Mr Philpot stood up and said more to the whole room than to us, 'Well, boys, you have a great plan with fabulous scientific concepts in place. I'm confident your rocket will perform well.'

He said it the way us kids say our lines when we are in a school assembly. Then he asked to see us outside.

'Dihydrogen monoxide?'

Mr Philpot raised an eyebrow once we were all outside. 'That is not the scientific name for water. It's an Internet hoax. Be careful what you're learning, boys. Now, I wasn't born yesterday, so I caught on to the fact that you were trying to impress the others. As you can see, I made a point not to embarrass you in front of them because the rest of the things you said were quite impressive, but let me tell you one thing right now, kids ...'

We listened, faces red with shame.

'Anyone who ever got anywhere in life did it with passion and drive, NOT with the sole purpose of impressing others. Do things for the right reasons, and that's the only way you can win.'

I kicked myself for not knowing that dihydrogen monoxide isn't the chemical name for water. My parents always call it water, even when we are using it on *Science Sundays*. If it had a fancy name, my parents would be the first to stick it into sentences and they would make sure I knew it. Just like I knew the formula for water is H_2O and named my imaginary dragon after it.

'That was pretty deep, what Mr Philpot said,' Daniel thought out loud, back inside the classroom.

He scribbled it down on a

piece of paper, announcing he was going to stick it up on his bedroom wall.

DO THINGS FOR THE RIGHT REASONS

'Yeah, and it was really cool of him to not shame us in front of the whole class,' whispered Charlie, looking around to make sure nobody was eavesdropping.

'Yep, it made his likability rating go way higher than the zero it was on before.' I chuckled.

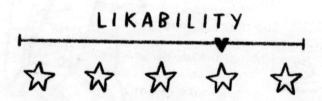

LIKABILITY

CHAPTER 8

We had Dad get us all the stuff we needed to

test our rocket:

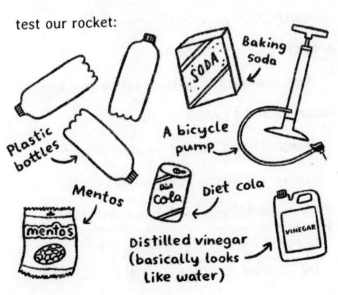

Baking soda

Plastic bottles

A bicycle pump

Mentos

Diet cola

Distilled vinegar (basically looks like water)

We had three different types of rockets to test.

Charlie arrived, wearing his bicycle helmet.

The kind that looks like a motorbike helmet.

'We'll need this for protection

from unexpected flying

objects.' He grinned.

'No. Expected flying objects. We're going to

make them fly! I hope,' I said.

Daniel arrived with a bag of broccoli,

cauliflower, cabbage and a tin of beans. 'I want

to see what happens if we stick all this in a

rocket and burn it. Will it work as powerfully as

it does in a human body?'

'Ermmmm. Daniel. I don't think that will work,' said Charlie.

'**Yes, it will,**' said Maryam, who would definitely be hanging around to annoy us today. But she got a stern look from Mum, because Mum knew that she knew that it wouldn't work and she knew that Mum knew that she knew.

We ran into the garden to go and set up while Mum explained sweetly to Daniel that plastic bottles can't **fart** as **grandly as him.**

Dad stood by with his phone to record videos of us.

And Esa and Mrs Rogers brought a bag of popcorn and sat down to watch from a safe distance.

We started off with the water rocket. It was easy to set up. We filled about a quarter of the bottle with water, put a cork in it and stuck the needle of the bicycle pump through the cork, so that we could pump air into the bottle. This would create so much pressure that the water would come bursting out with force and push the plastic bottle (our rocket) upwards.

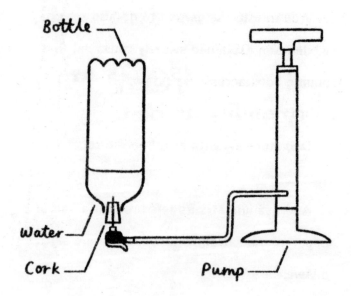

Charlie put on his
helmet and started pumping
while we stayed back. After
about ten pumps with his foot,
he called out, 'I don't think this is
working. Nothing's hap—'

WHOOOOOOOSH!

The rocket suddenly lifted off
towards the sky. **It was *EPIC!***

'OH MY GOSH!' Charlie screamed,
running back across the garden
towards us.

Everyone's eyes were on the
rocket.

'It went higher than the
house!' shouted Daniel.

'Awesome!' I said.

'Well done, boys,' said Dad.

'I am soooo proud of you!' said

Mum. 'I knew you could do it!'

We did it again and again, each having a

turn at pumping the rocket.

When it was Daniel's go, he pumped for a

while and then gave up. But when I went over

and gave it just two more pumps, it whizzed off

like Dad on his motorbike!

'Yeah, when the pumping gets harder and

you think nothing's happening, that's when it

shoots off!' I said.

'I love it!' said Charlie.

'Best day ever!'

Next, we tried the vinegar and baking soda

rocket, which ... didn't work.

We put the baking
powder and vinegar into
the bottle, put the cork
in, shook it around for a
second and ran for our
lives to watch from a
safe distance.

But nothing happened.

I turned to look at Mum. 'Why isn't it
working, Mum?'

Mum went to pick up the bottle carefully
and said that it was full of pressure. She forced
the cork off with her hands and the mixture
came bursting out.

'You need to play around with that one to see what's happening,' said Mum. 'Maybe the cork was on too tight, or maybe you need to create even more pressure with your reaction.'

We did. We played around with different amounts of vinegar and put the cork in tight enough so the vinegar didn't leak, but not so tight that the cork popped out.

AND iT WORKED!

Whoooosh went the

vinegar rocket, as

we clapped with

excitement.

Then we tried the cola and Mentos rocket, while Esa messed about with our bicycle pump.

That one was hard too because the Mentos reacted with the cola straight away, so we hardly had time to put the bottle upside down safely before **fizz was sprayed all over us.**

Esa wanted to know if he could drink the cola. But he wasn't allowed, super of course.

'Let's do the water rocket again!' I said.

I pumped and pumped away, expecting it to whoosh off any second, but nothing happened and my leg was getting tired. Something wasn't right.

Dad walked over to see what was going on.

'Oh. I can hear the air escaping when you're pumping,' he said. And looking more closely, he discovered that there was now a hole in the tube of the pump.

'ESSSSSSAAAAAAAAA!' I yelled.

Esa went to hide behind Mrs Rogers, who made a show of being his bodyguard if needed.

'Well ... I liked the water one the best,' said Daniel.

'Definitely. It went the highest and was the easiest not to get wrong ... as long as we have a working pump.' Charlie giggled.

'So we know which one we'll be making for the mini competition at school.' I nodded, hope bubbling up inside me.

CHAPTER 9

We spent our next two sessions perfecting

our rocket and designing the way it looked,

including adding cardboard bits to the bottle

so it flew better through the air. The fancy

word for that is

Daniel was really helpful with the design,

because he's amazing at crafts and drawings

and figuring out how to get stuff to stick to

other stuff. Sometimes he does it without glue by sliding the materials in ways I never would have thought of.

I carefully carried our test rocket to school on the day of the mini competition.

Mr Philpot had been having meetings with the three groups from the other classes too. He was going to judge which group got to go to MXF Labs for the national competition, based on how much the kids in the group knew the science and how well their test rockets worked.

After registration, all the classes met in the playground to watch the mini competition with their teachers and Mr McLeary. There were lots of faces staring, which made Charlie and Daniel act funny and gave me **wobbly knees.**

But our rocket looked good.

We had made it more
aerodynamic than the simple
bottle one we tested in the
garden. This one had a cone-
shaped nose and fins at
the bottom. All made
with light materials so
the rocket wouldn't
get too heavy to
lift off.

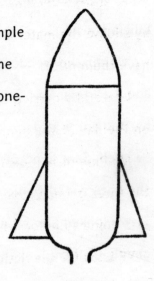

Mr Philpot was telling each of the groups
where to put their rockets down for the launch.
He was pointing at spots on
the ground with his giant
sandals, which was such a
funny sight it made me
giggle and loosen up a bit.

'Look,' said Charlie. 'One of the groups has Ellie's cousin, Sam.'

'Ohhhh, no wonder she's been so weird about all this. She **LOVES** Sam and wants her to win!' I said.

'Well, Sam's rocket looks all right. What if she does win?!' Daniel worried.

We looked around at the other rockets. A couple of them looked a bit like they would fall apart if they had to move, but Sam's was looking like it could win. Sam was smiling over at us like she knew it would. She had fangs, like a vampire, because that's how my brain made me imagine her.

Vampire, I thought.

But it was time for **blast off!** And in that moment, magically, we didn't care about the staring faces. We really just forgot they were there. We were only just showing everyone something we had fallen in love with – our rocket!

Everyone excitedly counted down,

'Five... Four... Three... Two... One... **blast off!**'

Charlie was pumping ours, which whooshed off awesomely, like we had hoped. We stood back and admired its flight. One group was covered in cola as their rocket fizzed and leaked in their hands, and the other two rockets, including Sam's, sat quietly on the

ground like stubborn toddlers who didn't want
to go home from the park.

Everyone was clapping for us.

Mrs Hutchinson looked super proud. Even
prouder than when Charlie got fifteen out of

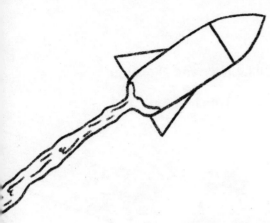

fifteen in his maths test. Her

magical hair was doing things I

was seeing for the first time. It was

as if her hair had goosebumps. And Mr

Philpot had a new air about him too.

'It's just amazing!' said Mrs Hutchinson.

'I'm so proud!'

'I'm not surprised. You know this science

and your rocket really well. Well done indeed,

boys,' said Mr Philpot to us.

'You're going to MXF Labs!'

Mr McLeary walked over and shook our hands, as if we were astronauts back from a space mission.

I couldn't even look at the other groups, because I felt sad for them. They must have wanted to go to MXF Labs just as much as we did. Sampire didn't look so fangy any more. She just looked the way a plant does when it hasn't been watered.

And that's probably why, back in the classroom, Ellie bounded up to us with Sarah close behind and said, 'OOOH, aren't we special?!'

'Yes, even Daniel is smart now, Ellie,' said Sarah. But she was doing upside-down talking, where she didn't mean what she was saying and everyone knew it.

'What's your problem?' asked Daniel crossly. 'Just be quiet and go and sit in your stinky corner.'

He was right. The corner that they sat in was stinky. Well, sometimes it was. Once in a while, there was a whiff of stinkiness through a vent above the table. Maybe it was coming from the school kitchen on days when cabbage was being cooked.

Cabbage was in one of the top spots on Daniel's list of highly 𝕱𝖆𝖗𝖙-POWERED FOODS and also his list for stinkiest foods, along with boiled eggs. The whiff didn't happen every day, but often enough that the kids sitting in that corner were known for it. Sarah and Ellie had begged others to swap seats with them for months, but nobody would.

SUPER OBVIOUSLY.

Ellie was livid at Daniel for that remark.

'You be quiet and sit in YOUR stinky corner!' She crossed her arms furiously.

But our corner wasn't stinky, and she knew it, which made her mad.

'Actually.' Sarah crossed her arms too. 'It can be their stinky corner, if they are brave enough to put their rocket where their mouth is.'

'What are you talking about?' said Charlie.

'Do you think your rocket will win?' Sarah asked.

Maybe. Probably. I hope so, I said in my own head. But out loud we all said, 'Yes!'

The whole class was watching now.

'Well, if you win, we'll never bother you again, but if you lose ... we get your corner, and you get ours.'

'You're on!' said Daniel.

And just like that, it wasn't only about getting a tour of a real rocket any more. We had to win, or we'd be sitting in the stinky corner for the rest of the year.

CHAPTER 10

After one last weekend of testing, we were all

set with our bits and pieces to go to MXF labs.

Mr Philpot had said parents didn't have to join

the kids going to Surrey for the competition,

but if they wanted to, one parent per group was

preferred. Everyone decided Mum should go,

which I was super happy about, because Mum

is what they call a *go-getter.* If she wants

something, she focuses and tries her best. Plus

she had been super helpful with our rocket,

always knowing what to tweak when it wasn't working well.

'You'll do great!' said Dad, squeezing me tight, as we got ready to leave on the day.

'I really wish I could come too, Omar,' said Mrs Rogers. 'That weekend testing rockets was the most fun I've had in a long time, since your dad doesn't let me zipline in the park any more.'

Even Maryam said, 'Yeah, it was actually pretty fun.'

But when I gave her a happy grin that said, *oh, so you love me?*, she quickly added, 'But I'm sure you'll find a way to flop.'

I gave her a big hug anyway, and tickled Esa before hugging him tight.

Charlie and Daniel were waiting in the Peanut, our massive 4x4 with a funny number plate, eager to set off.

The building we were staying in was a giant mansion. It was part of the huge MXF site, with its huge grounds and a separate building for the lab. The mansion building smelt of wood. I imagined that it belonged to little wood elves, who were actually right there, but camouflaged.

There were lots of big rooms inside with bunk beds where us kids would be sleeping. The parents and teachers got their own private rooms, which even had TVs in them. **SUPER NOT FAIR!** But I LOVE bunk beds, and I was excited about having a mega sleepover with Charlie and Daniel and the other competitors, who I was sure we would make friends with as soon as we met them.

Boy, was I wrong.

We were shown our bunks by a woman with a **RAZOR-SHARP FRINGE,** cut as straight as the side of a ruler, just above her eyebrows. She took small steps, but very quick ones, which sort of made it look as if she was going really fast, even though she was still walking at the same speed as my normal steps.

The other four boys staying in the room were already there, and as soon as the sharp fringe lady walked out, they surrounded us like a pack of hyenas.

One of them had the longest legs I had ever seen on a human, but with a really small top half. He reminded me of a cool-looking insect. His eyes were tiny, as if they belonged to the face of a much smaller kid like Esa. He was the one that shoved Charlie's shoulder.

'Who's the brains in your group? Is it you, red?' he said, referring to my friend's hair colour.

'No, it's him, tall,' said Charlie. Yikes! Where was the fish impression when you needed one? I was terrified Charlie would send the insect kid into a rage with his fast wit. And the HIM he was referring to was ME!

'Erm ... we're all the brains,' I said, holding my breath as 'tall' took a step closer to Charlie. Daniel angrily took a step between them, which they found hilarious.

'You can't all be brains. Marcus is the brains in this group,' said another of the kids in the circle around us, who was clearly the ringleader. He pointed to a kid who was everything you would imagine if someone asked you to describe a stereotypical smart person. Neat hair. Thick glasses. Simple clothes.

The ringleader was oozing confidence. He stood like he owned the room and everything beyond it. Even I started to feel like he was the boss of me as he went through the rest of the boys, pointing out why they were important.

'Jerad is the techy. He knows his way around gadgets like nobody you ever met, including the dude that discovered Apple.'

I knew what Charlie was dying to say. But I goggled my eyeballs his way, willing him to stay quiet. From the corner of my eye, I could see Daniel's face beginning to match his red top. Was he going to explode?

The ringleader smoothly carried on, 'The tall guy is called Bo, he's, you know, the muscles.

And I'm Liam. I'm the guy who makes sure we win.' He finished with a flick of his blond hair and a sinister curling of the lips.

They were like something from the movies. A group that's been put together to steal the world's biggest diamond. Except this time, the diamond was the rocket tour, and, well, I really wanted it to be ours.

The door opened and the fringe lady said, 'Time for dinner. Make your way to the hall now, please.'

We waited for the other boys to run ahead, then slowly sulked down the fancy carpeted stairs.

'Apple wasn't discovered! **It's not gravity!**' said Charlie.

'I knowwww!' I smiled because I knew how long he had been holding that in.

'And you don't need a techy for rocket science,' said Daniel.

'Yeah!' Charlie and I agreed.

'Or do you ...?' I wondered out loud. These boys had really messed with our heads. I was scared they were going to win.

But even after all of that they weren't the **scariest** group we were competing against ...

CHAPTER 11

Dinner was in a big hall with screens and a stage. This would be our introduction to the whole event.

We found my excited mum and Mr Philpot, who had arrived by train, on our round table, which had lots of seats free.

I made a quick dua to Allah that the boys from our room wouldn't sit there. And they didn't, but what sat there was even more terrifying.

It was a group of three girls. *Identical triplets.*

They walked over as if it was a rehearsed dance move and each chose a chair to sit on. One of their long dangly purses caught on Daniel's shirt sleeve as she sat down.

'Oh. Sorry. It's such a nice shirt as well, for a supermarket brand.' She smiled, with giggles from her sisters.

Daniel leaned over and whispered in my ear, 'I don't get it. Does she think it's a nice shirt or not?'

'No idea,' I whispered back.

Charlie found a printed menu on the table and decided to read it to us.

'For starters, there's a ... a ... quinoa salad,' he said, pronouncing it *kwin-o-ah.*

There was an eruption of giggles from the girls.

'Oh, that's cute.' One of them smirked, as if it wasn't cute. 'It's quinoa... Keen-wah.'

'So what's your rocket plan?' one of them asked.

'It's a water rocket,' I said proudly.

'Water? Oh, they're so cute, aren't they?' they asked each other deviously.

'Is "cute" the new slang for "really clever"?' asked Daniel.

'I don't think so ...' I blushed, glancing over to see what Mum thought. But she and Mr Philpot were busy chatting away.

'Anyway, we are **Gina, Gira and Giva.** You can call us **3G,**' they said and started chattering among themselves before we could even say our names.

As we got served our fancy food, a man walked on to the stage with the biggest smile ever and started speaking into the mic.

'Hi, everyone! It's so exciting to have you join us today!' He did really look happy about it. 'I'm Levi Bates, one of the scientists who worked on the MXF Labs H8 rocket. I'll be taking care of you during the competition tomorrow.'

Levi Bates carried on telling us more details, but as he spoke, the mic stopped working. He tapped it a couple of times and then laughed at himself, not feeling silly about it at all. He just spoke extra loud instead and said, 'Well, the rocket scientist can't figure out a microphone!' Everyone laughed and I liked him more because of it.

Then another lady came on called Ms Gelad, who was the top boss at MXF Labs, the CEO. She said a few boring details about safety and expectations from competitors. The audience didn't seem to like her as much.

Then Levi Bates spoke again. His smile hadn't left his face since he stepped on stage.

'Before you leave to rest for the night, I have a surprise announcement. It's an additional challenge. An extra boost that could help you win, and I am POSITIVE you will be just great at it! Every group must select a member to do a presentation about their rocket!'

He said this as if he had just handed each of us £1,000. Didn't he realise kids HATED speaking out loud in front of hundreds of people?!

'YES! It's going to be great!' He clapped. He made it sound so good that everyone, including me, clapped along with him.

'I want to do it. I'll present our rocket,' said Daniel.

And from the moment he said that, my heart was in my bottom,

because even though I hated myself for it more
than ever, I didn't think it would help us win.
Especially not when we were up against Liam
and his gang and 3G!

CHAPTER 12

We said good night to Mum and Mr Philpot.
Mum whispered in my ear to not worry about
the other kids. She must have also noticed the
weird girls. I gave her a hug and walked back
to our room with Daniel and Charlie.

'Those girls are so confusing!' said Daniel.

'Yeah, they're *nicey-MEAN*,' said Charlie.
'I think I prefer Sarah and Ellie. At least we
know when they're being mean!'

'I mean, I don't know if I'm cute and am

wearing a nice top, or if I'm repulsive and my top is too,' wondered Daniel.

'And 3G.' I giggled. '5G is the thing now. They need two more of them,' I said.

'No way, let's not have more of them!' Charlie giggled.

I imagined hundreds of them coming towards us and it was a scary sight.

We avoided Liam and his friends as much as we could, which was a bit like walking on your lips instead of your feet.

'Good night, little boys,' said Bo. 'Want Mummy to tuck you in?'

'Let them sleep, Bo. They'll need all the rest they can get to even come close to beating us tomorrow,' said Liam.

We stayed quiet, but Charlie flashed his torch at me three times, which meant:

those boys are bogs.

The next morning, after breakfast, all the groups were shown where they would be working outdoors. There were two people dressed in rocket costumes, walking around the area. The kind where you wonder how

the person inside can see where they are
going, because you can't see their face at
all. I guessed they were the mascots for the
competition.

My heart did a little flip
when I saw that we were
between 3G and Liam's
group. It was like being
the filling in a mouldy
bread sandwich. Charlie
and Daniel weren't so happy

about our neighbours, either. 'I'd rather work
with my underpants on my head all day than
work near these lot,' said Daniel quietly.

'I'd rather eat keeeeeeeenwaaaaah for
breakfast, lunch and dinner,' said Charlie.

'Come on, boys. We're going to have to zone

them out and get on with it,' encouraged Mum.

'Yup. We have to win, unless we want to sit in the stink zone for the rest of the year!' I said. But secretly, I cared less about the stink zone and more about the rocket tour.

'Yeah!' said Charlie and Daniel.

So we got geared up to build what we had practised loads of times last week.

Mr Philpot tripped over his own sandal's buckle on his way over to us, which didn't make us look any cooler in front of the others. I swallowed my embarrassment, which had formed into a big, sticky throat invader.

'Oh! Now we're going to build THE rocket. We have to name it,' said Charlie.

'Right!' I said.

'How about Turbo?' said Daniel.

'Boost?' added Charlie.

'*Madame Penelope*.' Daniel

laughed.

I grinned. 'I love all of them ... but ...

hmm ... it has to be something none of the

other groups would think of. Let's write down

something about our rocket, like what it would

do, or ... anyway, you get what I mean.'

So we got scribbling, and while we were doing

it, 3G started to linger around our space,

saying, 'Oh, do you know this competition will

be in the newspaper? There will be a photo

of the winning group. But don't worry, they

will definitely write the names of the ... ahem

... losers, too. Not saying that will be you, of

course.'

'What? I can't hear you. Seems to be bad reception,' I said, winking at my giggling friends and playing it cool, even though what they said terrified the flying saucers out of me.

They didn't get the joke, but they went off anyway.

'Let's see what everyone wrote,' I said.

We looked at our words and numbers and came up with a super-cool name for our rocket:

K4M1L

K for kinetic energy, which is the type of energy moving things have.

4 for the four main parts of our rocket: the pump, bottle, water and air.

M for miles, because we hope it flies miles high.

1 for first prize (hopefully).

L for lift offfff!

'Coooooool!' we said, very proud of ourselves.

Levi Bates came over, finger-combing his

silky blond hair away from his eyes, and smiling as huge as ever. His teeth looked like they belonged in a toothpaste advert. I imagined him on a poster at the dentist's.

I was actually super excited about meeting a real-life rocket scientist, especially one who had worked on the glorious H8 rocket! I would have to make sure that I didn't say anything stupid in front of him.

'Ah, a bicycle pump! I can see that you're going for a water rocket design! That's an excellent choice.' He smiled even wider, if that was even possible.

Charlie and Daniel stared at him, and I managed a small, 'Yes.'

He had a yucky-looking green smoothie in his hand, which he took a sip of and continued smiling, now with slightly green teeth. It made me realise he was just a guy. An extra-brainy, super-cool guy, but just a guy.

'Yes, they've tested out other models too,' said Mum proudly.

'Good! And you've tested different amounts of water to see what works best?' he asked.

We all nodded.

'That is SUPER,' said Levi Bates. 'Good luck!'

'What a nice man,' said Mum, as he walked off to talk to another group. 'That was a helpful thing to suggest.'

'Yes, I want to be him when I grow up,' said Daniel. 'Minus the green drink.'

'Me too,' I agreed.

Charlie was quiet. 'I don't know ... I've met better people,' he said. And of course, Daniel and I jumped on him, demanding to know what he meant.

But Charlie couldn't explain.

CHAPTER 13

It was time for the scrapyard challenge, which
was kind of scary. We were allowed to use
things like bicycle pumps from home, but for
the rest of the materials we needed to make our
rocket, we would have to rummage around in a
heap of recycled stuff. All the groups would do
it at the same time and we just had an hour!

'Good luck, everyone! Th*i*nk smart!'
Levi Bates winked with a flash of snow-white
teeth.

All the groups ran to the piles of materials.

We scanned for similar stuff to what we had built our test rocket with at home. I picked up a plastic bottle, just the right size, and began to feel less nervous. Maybe we would find everything we needed.

Liam walked casually over with Marcus and poked my bottle. 'Plastic is so basic. Who would make a rocket with a plastic bottle? Are you stupid or something?' he asked.

'Mrs Omar's mummmmmm! Liam called us stupid,' said Daniel.

'I didn't call them stupid. **I asked**

if they were stupid, ' Liam said flatly to my gobsmacked mum.

'Just ignore them,' said Mum after they turned around. 'People who put others down only do it because they are insecure about themselves. I'm sad for them, really.'

I got what she meant, but I couldn't be sad for them.

'Marcus, look for a metal bottle. Metal is best,' said Liam.

'Actually ... metal is too heavy—' Marcus started to explain, but Liam just glared at him like he had said that dogs have seven legs, and stomped away.

We found foam and card for our rocket fins and collected some paper clips, plastic wine glasses and pipes.

Levi Bates was wading through the bits and bobs, picking up materials and putting them down with a smile. Always a smile.

Mum said to ask him the things about building real rockets that I had always wondered. 'Now is your chance, darling. When will you meet a real rocket scientist again?!' she pushed.

So I took a deep breath. 'How long have you been making rockets?'

Levi looked at me, locking me in, as if I was the only one that existed on Earth and I had just asked the most important question that had ever been asked. He told me all about how he fell in

love with the mystery of the universe when his nan got him a telescope for his ninth birthday. Levi wanted to help the human race discover amazing things about it, so he went on to study a degree at university all about building rockets.

He made me feel so special that I wanted to ask him another question just so he would do it again, but Daniel beat me to it. Levi looked at Daniel in the same way, smiling the whole time, and answered his question about whether **{f@r+-POWERED FOODS** could ever make a human lift off a chair.

Then he said, 'Oh, interesting. You collected wine glasses,' and winked at Charlie.

'Yes, we're going to cut off the stem and use it as the nose for the rocket,' said Charlie.

'Oh, now that is smart!' Levi said.

'Thank you.' We smiled.

'You're very welcome. I'm **POSITIVE** you will do well here,' he said. Then Levi smiled, as if he had just remembered to. 'And I want you to.'

'Yeah, I really don't like that guy,' said Charlie as Levi Bates and his spotless white trainers headed off.

'Whaaaaaat? Why?' I asked.

'He is LITERALLY the nicest man I've ever met,' said Daniel.

'Maybe he just reminds you of someone you don't have good memories of?' tried Mum.

'Hmm ... no, I don't think that's it,' said Charlie.

The hour for scrapyard hunting was up,

so everyone was asked to go back to their workspaces. The rocket mascots came to shake our hands. They were silent, like those costumed mascots usually are. I used to be scared of them when I was little. I think my parents have a photo of me crying and running away from a giant panda.

We could see Levi Bates over in 3G's area. It looked like he was telling them something

about their rocket, so we eavesdropped a bit.
Yes, I know we shouldn't have ... but we really
wanted to know if he was giving them extra
winning tips!

'With the vinegar rocket, did you try
different amounts of vinegar?'

'No, sir,' 3G chimed together.

'Ah! Well, here's the trick! With less vinegar
in your bottle, the reaction will take longer.
But more pressure is created by the CO_2 gases,
which results in a larger thrust, sending your
rocket higher!'

'Oh my gosh, he's telling them the secret
trick!' I gasped.

'Whaaaaaat? Why?' Daniel shouted.

'Well, he did help us too,' said Mum.

Everyone was doing so well. I was happy for

them ... sort of ... maybe not for Liam's gang

... but man, I wanted ours to be the best. And I

still had to break it to Daniel that I didn't think

he should do the presentation. I didn't want

to hurt his feelings and make him think that

I agreed with Sarah and Ellie that he wasn't

smart enough. But I had to choose between

upsetting my friend and winning.

CHAPTER 14

We had a couple of hours before lunch to put our rockets together using the materials we had collected. Ours was looking pretty all right. I gave it one more tummy-rumbling happy look before we went off for our food fuel.

Lunch was outdoors, a few minutes' walk away from the workspaces. There were tables full of sandwiches, crisps, fruit and drinks that we could help ourselves to.

Levi Bates was sitting with a big, thick

science book that he closed when he saw us all gathering for lunch.

'Great book!' He smiled. 'I just finished it.'

'Oh, I have that one too,' said Mum. 'But it was only published the day before yesterday. You've already finished it?'

'Yes! **I'm a speed reader.** I can read over three thousand words a minute, with complete comprehension.' He smiled widely.

'Wowwww!' Daniel and I said. 'Cool!'

But when we piled tuna and cheese sandwiches on to our paper plates, Charlie said, 'I'm telling you, there's something not right with that guy. I overheard him telling some kid that he swam a ten-mile river marathon.

Who can do that? And read at three thousand words a minute? It's like he has Lamborghinis for eyes!'

'There's something not right about this sandwich. It smells like **mutant bananas,**' said Daniel, holding up a soggy-looking white bread mess.

'Ewwwww,' I said. And then back to Charlie, 'Don't worry, Charlie, I think he's OK.'

'I'm going to go find a quiet spot to pray,' said Mum.

'I'll help her. Because I know if she prays, God might help us win,' said Daniel.

'That's so kind.' Mum beamed.

And as soon as they went off, Liam, Bo, Jerad and Marcus slid over to us like snakes through grass.

'You!' Liam pointed at Charlie. 'Catch this!'
And Bo threw his backpack at Charlie.

Charlie actually did catch it, but it was so
heavy, he went straight down, face in mud and
bottom up in air.

'What's the matter? Too weak?' Liam smiled.

Where have I seen that smile before? I
wondered as I helped my friend
off the floor. Then I saw his
sad, muddy face and I felt
a hotness in my head that
I hadn't felt since the time
I saw a teenager snatch a lady's
bag and scoot off with it. I wanted to ram my
head into Liam's belly like in the videos of
people fighting in the street, but I knew I didn't
want to be them, because they always looked

terrible and out of control. So I breathed out, took Charlie's arm and stomped off, muttering to myself.

'Oh Allah, am I allowed to wish something really, really bad happens to someone? And if I do, would you do it? Because ... because ...

I **really** want Liam
to have an
uncontrollable
liquid poo episode in public!'

This made Charlie burst into giggles. It always makes me laugh when Charlie laughs with his toothy happiness, so I did too.

But when Daniel came back without Mum and asked what happened to Charlie's face, he said, 'What the baboon's red bottom?! Now I'm really angry!'

'It's OK, Daniel. I'm fine,' said Charlie. 'It's just a bit of mud.'

'No, it's not fine. We should teach them a lesson,' said Daniel. 'I know! While everyone's away from their areas for lunch we should go and do something to **mess up their rocket!** You just know they will cheat if they get the chance and we can't let them win!'

'Yeah, especially by cheating,' said Charlie.

'But messing up someone's rocket. That's sort of bad,' I said, because I knew I should. But I wanted to mess up their rocket as badly as Daniel.

'Don't worry, we will do it in a way that nobody finds out,' Daniel reassured him.

'What would we do to it?' asked Charlie.

'Just thump it hard. Break it to bits,' Daniel

said in a *duh, that's obvious* way.

'Hmmmm. I don't know ...' I said.

I felt myself dangerously close to giving in.
Was I really going to agree to destroy another
group's hard work? But the group was the
spawn of Shaytan himself, so it wasn't as bad
as breaking an innocent group's work, was it?
We might even be heroes for doing it, I told
myself.

'If my mum or Mr Philpot find out,
we're cat food.' I gulped. 'Besides,
we might not even be able to do
it. There might be people around
that could see us.'

'Look around!' said Daniel. 'Literally
everyone is here for lunch.'

So we walked back over to the workspaces

super casually. Daniel was right, they were completely deserted. Nobody was around. We could have done anything.

We walked over to Liam's gang's space and got a closer look at their rocket and all gasped. We couldn't believe what we were seeing. It was absolutely amazing! Like a gazillion times better-looking than ours. It was made out of special bits of metal, and had a tiny digital screen on the side, displaying funky maths equations.

'Right,' said Daniel, taking charge. 'Everyone make a circle and hold it together as high as we can, then at the count of three ... we drop it ...'

We did as he said. Hearts thumping hard.
This was the first crime we were going to
commit together. Then we would literally be

PARTNERS IN CRIME FOR EVER...

CHAPTER 15

'One ... two ...' Daniel counted.

I felt sick. Like a rocket of vomit was going to whoosh up my throat at any second.

'Three!'

I CLOSED MY EYES, ti9ht.

Nothing happened.

I opened my eyes. We were all still holding on to the gang's rocket tightly.

And when we realised, we all did the same thing and burst into giggles.

'I just couldn't do it!' said Daniel.

'Me neither!' said Charlie.

'It's too good to break!' I grinned.

We quickly put it down and ran-walked out of there.

'I mean, if those guys win, I think they deserve it,' said Charlie.

'Yeah!' we agreed.

On our way back to the lunch tables, we saw 3G walking back to the workspaces. If you can call the way they move 'walking'. It was super creepy, as if a villain and a ballerina had had triplets.

'And where exactly are you guys coming from?' one of the Gs demanded. I couldn't remember if she was Gina, Giva or Gira.

'Have you been messing around with our rocket?' they questioned.

'We would never do that,' I said, with the sweetest smile I could manage.

'Yeah! It's a little something we call integrity,' said Charlie.

'Everyone calls it that!' said one of the Gs and they evil-walked-slash-danced away.

'I'm still starving, I'm going to go and get some more food.' I grinned.

'Me too!' said Daniel.

But Charlie couldn't relax. 'I ate quite a lot of the **mutant-banana-flavoured** sandwiches. Turns out it's a flavour I like!' he joked. 'So, I'm going to go keep an eye on 3G to make sure they don't mess up our rocket, while you two go and eat.'

'OK, 007, good luck. Don't let them see you!' Daniel winked.

And Charlie ran off to be a spy.

After the break was over, we found Mum and headed back to our space. Mr Philpot was waiting there too. Charlie ran over, panting from his spying and clearly bursting to tell us something, but not in front of the adults.

Mr Philpot inspected our rocket carefully. He turned it round and round in his hands, looking closely at each bit, as if it was a new discovery that had come out of the ground. I imagined it was a dinosaur tooth,

and Mr Philpot was a famous explorer who had dug it up in some faraway desert.

'It's looking great, boys. Do you know the exact measurement of water to use?' he asked.

'Yes, sir. Three hundred millilitres,' Charlie replied.

'Great. And who will give the presentation?'

I awkwardly froze at this question and turned only my eyeballs to see what Charlie was doing. But he was frozen too.

'Well?' said Mr Philpot. 'It's the part you have to prepare for next, so who is doing it?'

'I am!' said Daniel, looking at Charlie and me as if we had gone nuts. 'You said I would do it, remember?'

We had actually never said he could do it. In fact, I had said he couldn't do it, shouldn't do it.

But I had said it in my own head. And right then,
I still couldn't bring myself to say that Daniel
could do it. There was so much at stake! If we
lost, we would have to move to the stinky corner
and we'd miss our chance for a rocket tour. I
had to buy time. Just a bit more time to think!

'Their rocket is out of this world!' I said,
pointing past the funny mascots towards Liam's
workspace.

'What?' said Mr Philpot, annoyed by the
change in subject, but equally interested in
what I was saying.

We told him all about the rocket Liam's gang
had built. Mr Philpot and Mum both said that
it sounded like it was cool-looking, but was
probably too heavy to launch without using
a more powerful substance than the ones we

were allowed to use for the competition.

I didn't know if I felt disappointed or secretly relieved that it would fail. And I still felt sick in my stomach for being a bad friend to Daniel. Maybe I just needed to talk about it with Mum.

I took her arm and dragged her away from everyone.

'Mum, I don't know what to do. Daniel wants to do the presentation, but I'm scared he won't know what he's saying and then we won't win.'

'Hmm. And how will it make him feel if you don't let him do it?'

'Well ... I think it will make him feel bad because he'll think everyone thinks he's not smart ... even his **bEst fRiEnDs**.'

'And do you want to make your friend feel like that?' asked Mum.

'Nope.'

'I guess you just have to think about what would make you feel worse: making your friend feel like even you think little of his capability, or losing this competition.'

I don't know how Mum manages to make things so clear so easily, but it was super obvious when she put it like that. If I made Daniel feel bad, he wouldn't get over it quickly and maybe we wouldn't be friends any more.

But if we lost the competition, even though I was dying for a rocket tour, I wouldn't feel bad for long.

'I choose Daniel, of course. Any day,' I said.

'I knew you would.' Mum winked. 'If Daniel keeps being made to feel like he can't do things, he'll begin to believe it. And you boys have done incredibly well with this rocket and had so much fun that you'll have those great memories whether or not you win.'

'You're right, Mum. I can't wait to tell him,' I said, running back to our tables while Mum went to get herself a coffee.

But I couldn't right then, because as soon as I got back, Mr Philpot went off on a toilet break and Charlie finally let out what he was bursting to tell us from his spy mission:

'Levi Bates is sabotaging EVERYONE'S ROCKETS!'

CHAPTER 16

'He whaaaaaatttt?'

'Yes! I saw him with these two eyes,' Charlie said, pointing at them as if they were all the proof we needed.

'But Levi Bates is from MXF Labs. He wouldn't do that,' Daniel said.

'Yeah, and he was helping people, remember? He told 3G that less vinegar would make their rocket go higher. Why would he help the groups and then make their rockets fail?!' I asked.

'And he told us our wine-glass nose was brilliant. He cares!' said Daniel.

'No. Guys! Listen!' said Charlie, desperate. 'I saw him put water in the vinegar bottles.'

'So when all the vinegar rocket groups take their vinegar from there, it won't work ... because it will be water?!' I gasped.

'Genius,' said Daniel admiringly.

'Evil genius,' Charlie corrected.

I had liked Levi Bates A LOT but Charlie is

my best friend and he's no liar. I felt silly for not listening to his spidey-sense before.

Daniel believed him too. 'Let's tell someone,' he said.

'But nobody will believe us, will they?' said Charlie, hopeless eyebrows hanging on his face.

'I guess not. I mean, he's Levi Bates. He's from MXF Labs and who they chose to look after us,' I said.

'Do you have proof, by any chance?' Daniel asked. 'Other than your eyes, which can't really help us.'

'No. I don't have a phone, so I couldn't record it.'

'Well, then it's our word against his if we tell anyone,' I said.

'Yeah, and guess who they will believe?' said

Daniel. 'I'll give you a clue: he doesn't have red
hair, glasses and the best smile in the universe
... actually, he does sort of have the best smile
in the universe, doesn't he?'

'Ha ha ... his smile is pretty great,' I agreed.

'HEYYY!' said Charlie. 'He's evil, remember?'

'Sorry, it's just so hard to remember that.

He's also *super* awesome.'
I grinned sheepishly.

'Great! Nobody is going to believe me if
even you guys are having trouble seeing past
the nice-guy act!' wailed Charlie.

'Sorry, Charlie! I'll imagine
him as a big goblin with a
growly voice,' I said. 'But
not every group is using
vinegar, so maybe we can

follow him to see what else he does and try to record it?'

'Yeah, we can use your mum's phone,' said Charlie.

'And I think we should tell Mum too.'

'No, don't tell her!' said Charlie.

'Don't tell her what?' said Mum, suddenly appearing behind us, with an ever so tiny cappuccino moustache.

'Er, that you have coffee on your face,' said Charlie as innocently as possible.

Mum laughed and said that she wasn't born yesterday and made us tell her what was going on. I don't know why she bothered, **because she didn't believe us.**

'Oh, sweetie, he was probably just topping up the vinegar supply. You know I work in a lab and those bottles can sometimes look like water bottles. I can understand why you thought you saw what you did, but Levi Bates is an extremely well-respected rocket scientist – he really would have no reason to do something like that.'

And that was it. There was no point trying to make her believe. So using her phone to follow Levi Bates and catch him in action was out of the question, because she wouldn't let us do that.

'We'll need more people to help us. People with phones. But we also have to be careful about who we tell,' said Daniel.

'Hmm, but who will help us?' wondered Charlie, looking around.

I pointed. 'Look, guys! 3G have phones.'

They were recording little videos of themselves with their rocket, which was looking pretty good.

I couldn't believe it, but we were going to have to get the mean girls on our side, and we knew it wouldn't be easy.

CHAPTER 17

We acted casual in front of Mum for a bit,
pretending to focus on our rocket, and then
said we wanted to see if 3G were having as
much fun as us and went over.

'Hello,' I said, not knowing where to begin.

'Oh, how nice of you to visit us,' said Gina.
Again, sounding exactly like it was the opposite
of nice.

'We are here for a reason,' said Daniel
importantly.

'Yes, it's about Levi Bates.'

Charlie wasn't saying anything. He was going along with his *stay quiet, and they won't have anything to make fun of* policy.

'Oh, him. We HATE him!' they said all at once.

'You whaaaaaat?!' we shouted.

'He said our rocket was nice. Everyone knows when you say something is nice, it really means it's **completely basic.'**

Giva frowned.

'Hey, so when you said my shirt was nice ...'
said Daniel crossly.

Gira giggled happily. 'Uh-huh. Not nice.' And
then she flashed a sweet smile.

'And your trainers are nice. Very, very nice
actually!' said Daniel, trying hard to use the
word to be mean.

But we all giggled. 'No, if you say "very"
before "nice" then that means it's actually
nice,' explained Giva.

'OH MY GOSH. My brain will break with all
this **upside-down talking.**
Just say what you mean!' Daniel clapped a hand
over his face.

3G giggled again. 'OK, we'll try. So what's up with Levi Bates?'

We filled them in on what Charlie saw, and their jaws dropped wider and wider.

'So he's a fake!' they said.

'Exactly, he's slime disguised as candy floss!' said Charlie, excited that others shared his feelings about Levi.

'He's not going to get away with it. He's messed with the wrong triplets,' seethed Gina, looking more **sinister** than ever.

The rocket mascots hung around nearby and we tried to make sure they couldn't hear us while we quickly hatched a plan. Armed with 3G's three phones (of course, they each had one of the latest phones), we all had a role to play and a place to be.

During the discussion, I whispered to Charlie that we should tell Daniel that he would be doing the presentation.

'So, Daniel, you were right; you are doing the presentation.' I smiled.

'You'll be great,' Charlie's toothy mouth said.

'I know,' said Daniel, making me giggle once again.

Our plan to catch Levi Bates looked like this:

- Daniel was going to keep Mum and Mr Philpot busy by rehearsing his presentation with them (he was really excited about doing it, like a new Daniel with a sparkly skin).

- I was going to hide behind
the bins, with a view of the
rocket supplies.

- Charlie was going to walk
around casually with Gina.

- Gina was going to pretend to
rest on the grass right in the
middle of the grounds so she
could see who was coming
and going.

- Gina was going to stay at
their workspace in case
Levi Bates came around to do
something suspicious.

'We'll have caught him red-handed soon!'
said Giva.

But half an hour passed and we had
nothing. And that also meant we
were half an hour closer to
presentation time. The only
thing we caught Levi Bates
doing on camera was
Scratching his bottom when he
thought nobody was looking. Other than that,
he seemed as angelic as anyone could be.

I had spent the time hiding in my corner,
bored out of my brains and imagining how
Allah sees, hears and knows everything that
everyone does and keeps a record. I wished
I could borrow some of His records now to
show Levi Bates putting water into the vinegar

bottles earlier. But obviously, I couldn't do that.

I had thought about the time I had been in big

trouble for something I didn't do, and how, in

the end, the proof had come. I asked Allah to

make it come again. To show everyone what I

knew **He knew.**

THAT LEVI BATES WAS A

FAKE ROCKET DESTROYER.

CHAPTER 18

It was looking obvious that we wouldn't catch
Levi Bates doing anything, so we called another
secret meeting.

'Think, guys!' said Charlie, completely
freaking out. 'We have forty-five minutes until
everyone presents their rockets and they won't
work!'

'Hmm. What would you do next if you were
a charming, super-cool, super-smart, speed-
reading criminal mastermind with special

abilities?' I said, and got a cross look from Charlie, reminding me that I was supposed to be seeing him as a goblin.

'What else would he do to sabotage the other rockets?' thought Gira out loud.

'I've got it!' Daniel shouted and then whispered, 'The other rockets are using equipment kids have brought from home, like bicycle pumps for water rockets. The only thing he can do to stop a water rocket is to make a hole in the pump's tubes. Remember, guys, like Esa did during our tests?'

'YES! YOU'RE a GENIUS, DANIEL!'

I said to him. And I meant it. Daniel WAS smart. Maybe not at maths or at science, but he was a quick thinker and a problem solver for sure.

Daniel blushed pink.

Even 3G gave Daniel impressed congratulations, without a trace of sarcasm.

'So he's going to go to all the groups with bicycle pumps!' said Charlie.

'Let's go!' said Gina.

Off we went, while Daniel went back to our
table so Mum wouldn't come looking for us.
But before we knew it, he came panting back.

'Levi Bates was at our table while we were in
the secret meeting!' he gasped. 'Your mum told
me when I got back. Come on, he
might have done something!'

We ran back to
our rocket to test it out. And sure
enough, pump as we might, our spare water
bottle wouldn't lift off. Levi Bates had managed
to poke a hole into our pump while we were
away.

'Nowwwww will you believe us?' I said desperately to Mum.

'But maybe this is the one that had a hole in it from before? **Maybe you brought the wrong one?** We didn't test it out here.'

Mum thought so well of everyone, she would never see it, and we had no time to waste.

'Well, if nobody's rocket works, then nobody will win, and Ms Gelad will know something is wrong,' said Gira.

'But why would Levi Bates sabotage our rockets? It's so weird,' I said.

'Maybe he's helping another group win by killing everyone else's chances!' suggested Daniel.

'I guess we will soon find out!'

So our grand plan was to go ahead with the
show and wait to see whose rocket blasted
off without any trouble. We spent ten minutes
wondering where Mum was and watching Mr
Philpot panic that Daniel wasn't ready for the
presentation.

'He's been so distracted. What is going
on with you kids?' he demanded. But
he didn't look as scary as usual,
because one of his shirt buttons
had popped open where his belly
had popped open where his belly
was pushing against it.

'Erm, nothing, sir,' I answered.

And just then, five minutes before showtime,
Mum came running back to us, hijab out of
place and out of breath.

'I just had to check. I couldn't let it go

without making sure, so I went to
see the vinegar with my own
eyes and, well, I managed to
test the pH with the little bit
of it that was left with
these strips I have in my
bag, and ... and ...

Charlie's right...

it's water!' She held her throat, as if what she
had just said was going to make her vomit. I
knew the feeling really well.

   'Sorry?!' said Mr Philpot, who was hearing
of it for the first time.

   'We'll fill you in on the way!' shouted Mum.
'Follow me, everyone, let's go and find Ms
Gelad!'

   We ran as fast as we could to the

'launchpad'. But of course, we were too late.
Ms Gelad was on stage with Levi Bates and the
security guards said there was no way we could
get to Ms Gelad now, as she began her opening
speech into the mic.

CHAPTER 19

Ms Gelad was asking everyone to take their
seats, which had been laid out to view the
launchpad. It was basically a big stage that
had a big screen with awesome booming
speakers, hooked up. On it they were
showing a funky MXF Labs video of their own
rocket-building. Later all the groups would
show their presentation on it, if they had made
slides. We had. Mum was a pro at PowerPoint,
and Daniel had used his awesome artistic skills

to make our slides look super brilliant. He was very proud and extremely excited about presenting.

Mr Philpot was looking **furious,** now that he was filled in on what was going on. I hoped he would blow his top like a rocket and shout at Levi Bates. He led us huffily to our seats and we looked like baby ducklings in a row, following him.

I was the last duckling, and suddenly I felt a firm tug on my arm and heard a familiar voice.

'Follow me!'

I spun round to see one of the rocket mascots and my brain registered. It was Maryam's voice! I would know that voice anywhere. I've known it all my life! So, with a shocked, beating heart, I followed the mascot around the corner to a hidden spot where the other mascot was waiting. They both pulled off their headpieces. It was so UNREAL that I actually rubbed my eyes like I was a cartoon. The mascots were Dad and Maryam!

'HOW THE WHO?! WHAT THE WHEN AND WHO THE HOW?' I GASPED.

'I know this is a shock, son!' said Dad, holding me by my shoulders and then full-on hugging me tight. 'We'll explain everything later, but we know about Levi. All the proof is on a video on this **USB STICK**. We can't get on to the stage. It's up to you from here.'

'You can do it, Omar!' said Maryam. 'Now go!'

I ran back to join the others in the seats, my brain in overdrive and the USB held tight in my fist. All I knew was, I had to let Daniel have his moment and do the presentation. I couldn't do anything till then.

As I slid into my seat, with loud whispers from Daniel asking where I went, Ms Gelad was handing the mic over to Levi Bates. I couldn't

tell him or Charlie anything. Daniel wouldn't be

able to concentrate on his presentation. But I

was so nervous, my heart was flipping between

my stomach and my chest. I had to imagine

H_2O to keep me sane while I breathed through

it.

'It's time!' He was beaming. Teeth whiter

than ever.

whispered Charlie.

'Each group will launch their rocket in turn,

on this stage, and we have laser technology to

measure the height of the lift-off for each one.

As you know, we will also be awarding points for the presentation, which will show us how well you understood the science behind the rocket,' Levi explained.

'Yeah, except none of them will go very far, will they?' whispered Daniel.

'I can't wait to get started!' Levi Bates clapped, as H_2O glared at him crossly and held two little claws up behind his head as funny ears.

Liam's group went first. Liam did the presentation. He said lots of things, with the gallons of confidence he had, but he didn't actually say

anything that made sense for rocket science.
It was like a **magic trick** – he
rambled on about nothing much but still
impressed everyone. Then the group
launched their cool-looking rocket.
And to my surprise – it worked! It
shot off with a colossal whoosh
into the air.

Charlie, Daniel and I shot
looks at each other. So that was
the group Levi didn't destroy.
But why?

Another group went next,
and as we knew would happen, their rocket
didn't work. I felt so bad for the kids, who
looked panicked knowing everyone was
watching, as if they were guilty of something

terrible. The crime of failing. This made me **angrier and angrier.**

Levi Bates was the guilty one. I wanted to shout out to the kids on stage, 'It's not your fault!'

I saw Daniel's fists clenched tight with rage, so I put an arm round him and glanced over at Charlie. But he looked sad rather than angry, the corners of his lips trying to meet his chin. I was super glad only one more group was going on before us, and it was 3G, who knew what to expect.

3G stormed on, didn't bother to present properly and then tried to launch their rocket while shooting Levi Bates deadly looks. Then it was our turn. Daniel walked up the steps with pride. He really, really wanted to smash the presentation, even if the rocket didn't lift off. Charlie and I followed, and I put a hand on Charlie's shoulder because I felt dizzy from stress.

Daniel was amazing. He explained **Newton's third law** and gave examples from real life, like when you walk your foot pushes the ground and the ground pushes back, sending you forward. He explained about the water bursting out because of the pressure from pumping air in the bottle, and the water pushing hard downwards against the ground to send the rocket shooting upwards. He even explained how our rocket's design would make it fly better. He was like a teacher.

And he made everyone laugh. He was just

great. A natural. I felt like a **proud dad,**

even though I was trembling with nerves

because of what I had to do next.

While Charlie and Daniel were busy setting

up K4M1L, I stuck the USB in the computer and

took the mic in my shaky hands. With a deep

breath and an encouraging nod from H_2O, I let

the video of evidence play.

CHAPTER 20

On the big screen, a series of videos started
playing. They were of Levi Bates, going around
wrecking everyone's chances of winning.
There were clips of him breaking things in
the scrapyard challenge, swapping vinegar for
water, puncturing holes in pumps and shaking
people's cola bottles so they would lose the
fizz. It was all there for everyone to see.

'Allah?' Daniel said out loud, not
realising I had played it, and thinking it

was God directly letting us have some of
His records just like I had wished. I had
goosebumps all over. It was a weirdly epic
moment.

'I'm sorry, everyone! None of the other
rockets will work and you can see why!' I said
into the mic. **'Levi Bates sabotaged
everyone else!'**

'No! No! Turn this off!' Levi Bates was
shouting, his smile gone. 'AV team, turn this
nonsense off!'

Ms Gelad
looked properly
flabbergasted. Her
flabber was gasted
so much that she was
frozen on her spot.

The rocket mascots jumped on to the stage now, taking the remote to rewind the video evidence and play it again, happily.

'Give me that!' Levi pounced. 'How dare you? Who are you?'

The rocket mascots took their headpieces off and this time it was my group's

Flabber that was gasted

when they saw Dad and Maryam.

Mum and Mr Philpot dashed on to the stage too, and completely bombarded them with questions.

Daniel was doing a breakdance on the stage and singing, 'We got you. We got you gooood.'

'SECURITY!

Escort this ridiculous man

off the premises!' ordered Ms Gelad, finding her voice.

Security got hold of a very sheepish-looking Levi Bates.

'But wait. Why did you do it?' Charlie asked.

'My son. I needed him to win.'

'Liam is his son!' I pointed. They looked so similar that I couldn't believe we hadn't seen it before.

'Pardon me? Your son? That's against the rules. Your son is not even allowed to enter the competition,' said Ms Gelad.

'He wouldn't take no for an answer! And nobody at work knows him, so I thought it would be OK. Liam wanted me to help him make a winning rocket, the best rocket ... but he wouldn't listen to me or to his group. He wanted it to be all jazzy-looking. I knew it wouldn't lift off very high, if AT ALL, but if he didn't win, he would make my life miserable with his moaning. I just had to make sure he won so I could have some peace. So I used some of my own tricks and made sure nobody else's rocket would work, just as a back-up.' Levi Bates spoke as if his whole body was in pain.

And then he was marched away, never to be seen again.

Just kidding, he was seen again, but I've always wanted to say that. In fact, he was seen lots of times on Maryam's YouTube video. One million views in a week!

*

Mum wouldn't let go of Maryam; she was

hugging her so tight I thought she might

disappear. Then she suddenly jumped out of her

skin as if she'd just

remembered she had

three kids.

'Where's Esa!?'

'Relax, he's with

Mrs Rogers,' said

Maryam. 'We got here

early this morning.'

'We, ermm, stopped for these costumes on

the way so we could disguise ourselves. We

didn't want Mum to be annoyed that we tagged

along after all. We weren't trying to steal her

moment with Omar; we just wanted to see

him compete,' Dad explained, looking at Mum

through his eyelashes like he does when he doesn't know if she's mad at him. 'We went straight to reception to let them know we were here and would be wearing costumes. Ms Gelad thought it was a great idea.'

'Then we overheard Levi Bates on the phone being **VERY ShADY,** so we started recording his every move.'

'You're the best!' I said, trying to hug them both at the same time. 'But why didn't you tell us sooner?'

'Well ... Madam Maryam's phone was already full of videos and photos and wouldn't let her record any more, so we only had the evidence on my phone. But just as we caught him puncturing the tubes on the pumps, my phone died!' **Dad facepalmed.** 'So we had to rush around to find a charger.'

'Then we waited for the moment that would bring him the most shame. Here on the big screen in front of all the people affected by his devious plot!' said Maryam, posing like a secret spy agent.

We couldn't stop laughing with relief, and at how hilarious it was that Dad and Maryam had been there all day and recorded Levi Bates as funny rocket mascots. They were like the FBI, but cooler, I thought. They were cooler than anything.

Ms Gelad took the mic again and announced that though none of the rockets actually took off (apart from Liam's, which didn't count any more because of the cheating), she was able to assess which one would have been the most impressive. It belonged to 3G, who, you won't believe this, actually got on stage to do a winning dance they had prepared for weeks before. They had won tea with Conrad Arnett,

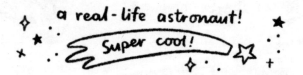

a real-life astronaut!

Super cool!

'BUT,' Ms Gelad said awkwardly, 'the rocket that would have reached great heights AND whose presentation was out of this world was

Group Omar, Charlie and Daniel!'

We couldn't believe it! We won the rocket
tour!

CHAPTER 21

For the first time since I'd met him, Liam
looked like he didn't know what to say. He
looked like bolts of electric fizz were
whirring through his bloodstream.

This time, Bo was grabbing his shirt
front, saying, 'Did you know about
this? Do you know how stupid your
dad has made us look?'

Jerad and Marcus were pulling
him off like some sort of comedy

on TV, Jerad tugging on Bo's waist and Marcus pulling on Jerad. Ms Gelad was also trying to get them to settle down and failing.

'Stop that, the four of you!' shouted Mr Philpot in his bellowing voice, which was enough to make a lion have a panic attack. They all stopped and stood to attention. Bo was saluting, with his hand to his head, which made us all scoff giggles back down our throats.

Then in a gentler voice Mr Philpot said to them, 'What happened is not Liam's fault. He didn't ask him to do it, so settle down.'

Liam hung his head and his electric wave body relaxed a bit. 'I guess I do push my dad's buttons ... but sometimes I feel like he's so busy building that H8 rocket that he doesn't even look at me unless I do crazy things.'

'Woah,' whispered Daniel. I got him. I got that so much. And so we all went to give Liam a slap on the back or a prod with an elbow to say that we weren't mad at him.

We did feel super bad for all the other groups who had rockets that didn't fly thanks to Levi Bates. Ms Gelad did too. But she had the amazing idea for an out-of-this-world treat for every kid that took part.

It made me even more excited than the tour of the H8 rocket. Ms Gelad said that she would make sure that when H8 went on an unmanned exploration to Mars, she would send a tiny little object from each group to leave there, right on Mars. Maybe the aliens would discover them? Or angels? Who knew?

'OH MY GOSHHHHHHH! Imagine, Omar. Something of ours in outer space! That's making me feel like I can do anything in the universe!' shouted Daniel.

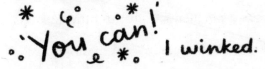

'You can!' I winked.

I was really happy to see my best friend feel that way about himself. Finally.

When we got home, Mrs Rogers was bursting to hear every detail. We had already phoned her from the car, of course, but she wanted to know EVERYTHING.

'Didn't you suspect anything before?' she asked.

'I did,' said Charlie proudly. 'I knew he wasn't right.'

'Yes, he was just so extremely charming. And NICE,' said Mum. 'I never would have thought.'

'He tricked everyone with his extra-smooth smoothness,' I told Mrs Rogers. 'And Dad and Maryam are heroes!'

Dad flexed his biceps and tried to lift Maryam on to his shoulders, which she was way too big for now. So she got dropped back down on to the sofa straight away, 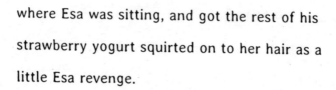 where Esa was sitting, and got the rest of his strawberry yogurt squirted on to her hair as a little Esa revenge.

I giggled happily as I looked at everyone's smiling faces.

My family, including Mrs Rogers, were definitely my happy place.

CHAPTER 22

Back at school, Mrs Hutchinson had prepared a surprise banner for us, which said:

The whole class gave us a standing ovation for winning, cheering and whooping and giving us high-fives. Even Sarah and Ellie came and shook our hands. They didn't get to swap seats with us and get out of their stinky corner, but they seemed kind of impressed by the YouTube video, especially Daniel's presentation.

'You were really brave, Omar.' Ellie smiled proudly.

'I watched the video soooo many times!' said Sarah.

Cool, that meant they'd probably stick to their promise of not teasing us any more. At least for a while!

'And who are those triplets? **They seem ... nice,**' said Ellie. There was a burst of giggles from us, now that we knew what that meant.

'They're actually quite cool.' I nodded my head.

'They're very, very nice.' Daniel nodded, with a wink at me and Charlie.

*

Mr Philpot and Mr McLeary also came in to say congratulations. I was blushing to see how proud the head teacher was of our group.

'Ms Gelad has asked us to send over your object for Mars,' said Mr Philpot. 'Have you thought about it?'

We had. We had talked about it on the phone. It had to be small and light, and we wanted to give the Martians the best piece of advice we had learned through the whole thing.

'Did you bring it?' Charlie asked Daniel.

'Yep!' said Daniel, reaching to his back pocket and pulling out a folded piece of paper. It was the paper from his wall with Mr Philpot's words on it:

DO THINGS FOR THE RIGHT REASONS

'We think maybe Mr Levi Bates' teacher didn't tell him that,' I said.

Mr Philpot blushed tomato red, and a little tear dropped out of his eye.

Mrs Hutchinson's curls wove around each other as if they were hugging.

'That's absolutely grand!' said Mr McLeary.

Oh, and we filled the paper with lots more advice, with a bit of help from Mrs Hutchinson and the rest of the class, just in case the Martians ever made it to Earth!

Learn how to tell if people are being *FAKE*. Come and take lessons from Charlie if you like!

Sometimes, 'NICE' means 'NOT NICE'.

Careful which Earth vegetables you eat – some of them are filled with fart power!

Please don't take our planet, like in the movies.

If you need a rocket to get here, Omar and his friends can make you one.

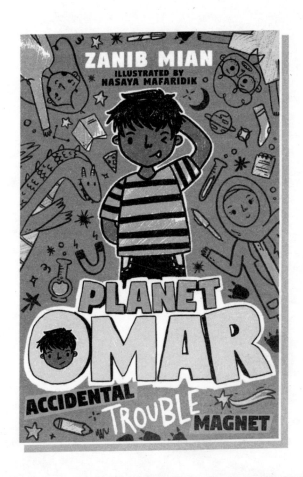

**WELCOME TO THE IMAGINATIVE BRAIN OF OMAR!
ARE YOU READY TO LAUGH SO HARD THAT SNOT
WILL COME OUT OF YOUR NOSE?**

**GET READY TO SOLVE AN EPIC MYSTERY
WITH OMAR AND HIS FRIENDS!**

ZANIB MIAN

ILLUSTRATED BY
NASAYA MAFARIDIK

PLANET OMAR

INCREDIBLE RESCUE MISSION

SOMETHING VERY STRANGE IS GOING ON
AT SCHOOL, BUT NOBODY SEEMS TO BE
TAKING IT SERIOUSLY — EXCEPT CHARLIE,
DANIEL AND (OF COURSE) OMAR!

THERE'S TROUBLE AT SCHOOL AND ONLY SUPER OMAR CAN SAVE THE DAY — BUT WHO WILL RESCUE HIM WHEN HE NEEDS HELP?

ZANIB MIAN grew up in London and still lives there today. She was a science teacher for a few years after leaving university but, right from when she was a little girl, her passion was writing stories and poetry. She has released lots of picture books with the independent publisher Sweet Apple Publishers, but the *Planet Omar* series is the first time she's written for older readers.

KYAN CHENG is currently residing in Bristol with her husband and furbaby pup. One of her favourite things to do growing up was drawing characters from books and TV shows. She now has fun creating her own characters and continues to explore her favourite themes which include nature, food and all creatures great and small.